GREAT ILLUSTRATED CLASSICS

A TALE OF TWO CITIES

Charles Dickens

adapted by
Marion Leighton

Illustrations by
Brendan Lynch

BARONET BOOKS, New York, New York

GREAT ILLUSTRATED CLASSICS

edited by
Malvina G. Vogel

Contents

About the Author

Charles Dickens was born in England, in 1812, the second of eight children of a debt-ridden government clerk. Because his family had handled their money poorly, young Charles was sent to work in a London factory at the age of ten. This experience upset him so greatly and left such an impression on him that he later created poor, suffering people as the heroes of many of his novels and cruel, selfish rich ones as the villains.

A small, unexpected legacy permitted Charles to break free of the slave factory and return to school. He became a newspaper reporter — a job which helped him to observe people and to create scenes that live in his readers' memories.

With the appearance of *The Pickwick Papers* in 1836 and 1837, Charles Dickens, at age 24, became the most popular novelist in England. This popularity increased with the publication of *David Copperfield, Oliver Twist, A Christmas Carol, Great Expectations,* and *A Tale of Two Cities.*

Dickens had a keen interest in politics and in improving social conditions. He used this interest to weave the exciting characters and events in France and in England that led up to the French Revolution in his historical novel, *A Tale of Two Cities.*

Much of Charles Dickens' life was spent writing, editing, touring to read his novels, and promoting many charities to help the poor. He was active in all this work until his death in 1870.

The Nobles and the Peasants

CHAPTER 1

The Mysterious Message

It was the year 1775, and both France and England were on the brink of revolution. King George III of England was too busy handling his country's problems with the American colonies to worry about his own people's poverty. King Louis XVI of France and the noblemen of his court were more concerned with their own pleasures and wealth to worry about the poor, hungry lower classes, who had begun to make plans to overthrow their rulers. So it was that London and Paris, the capitals of the two countries, were uneasy as their revolutions drew near.

There was much crime in England during this period. Thus it was not surprising that the passengers in the mail coach traveling out of London one Friday night late in November feared for their safety when the sound of a galloping horse came from behind the coach.

The guard cocked his pistol. "Stop or I shall fire!" he shouted.

The rider slowed down and stopped. "I must speak to one of the passengers heading for Dover," he called out. "Mr. Jarvis Lorry."

The guard turned to the passengers. "Which one of you is Mr. Lorry?" he asked.

"H-Here I am," replied a trembling gentleman of about sixty. "Who wants me?"

"It's Jerry Cruncher," answered the rider. "I have a message from Tellson's."

"Very well," Mr. Lorry told the guard. "I know this messenger. I work for Tellson's Bank in London, and so does he."

Mr. Lorry took the paper the rider handed into the coach. He unfolded it and read to

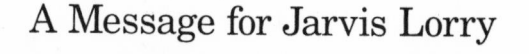

A Message for Jarvis Lorry

himself, "Wait at Dover for Mam'selle." Then he turned to the rider. "Jerry, you can say that my answer is 'RECALLED TO LIFE.' "

"That's a mighty strange answer," muttered the messenger as he climbed back onto his horse.

Mr. Lorry, meanwhile, began to doze, as did the other passengers. But his sleep was not a restful one, for his dreams were filled with scenes of him digging a man out of a grave.

Over and over Jarvis Lorry asked the ghost, "How long have you been buried?"

"Almost eighteen years," was the ghost's repeated reply.

"Do you know that you are being recalled to life?"

"They tell me so."

When these conversations became loud enough to waken the other passengers, they nudged Mr. Lorry awake. It was during one of these waking moments, in the black of night, that Mr. Lorry saw the other two passengers

Dreams of Digging a Man out of a Grave

leave the coach and walk off down the road.

By mid-morning, the mail coach arrived in Dover, the departure point for boats crossing the English Channel to Calais, France. Mr. Lorry arranged for a room at the Royal George Inn, in Dover, since the boat would not be leaving until the following afternoon. Then he told the innkeeper, "Please prepare another room for a young lady who will arrive today. She will ask for Mr. Lorry of Tellson's Bank."

"You gentlemen from Tellson's do quite a bit of traveling, don't you?" commented the innkeeper.

"Yes, we have offices in both England and France," explained Mr. Lorry, "but I have not done any traveling in fifteen years."

It was that evening, as Jarvis Lorry was finishing his dinner, that a waiter informed him that a Miss Manette had arrived.

Leaving his dessert unfinished, Mr. Lorry hurried upstairs. Entering Lucie Manette's sitting-room, he saw a young lady of no more

Arranging for Another Room

than seventeen. She was a short, slim, pretty girl with long golden hair and deep-set blue eyes that met Mr. Lorry's with a questioning look. That look made him recall a child whom he had held in his arms during a passage across the English Channel from France to England fifteen years before. He knew that she had been that child, but Lucie Manette, of course, did not recognize him.

"I'm pleased to meet you, Miss Manette," said Mr. Lorry, making a formal bow.

The young lady motioned Mr. Lorry to a chair and got right down to business. "I received a letter yesterday from Tellson's Bank, sir, informing me about a discovery... regarding some property of my poor father... who has been dead for so long. The property, I believe, is in France..."

Her voice trailed off, and she wiped away a tear, then struggled to continue. "The letter said I was to go to Paris to meet with a gentleman the bank was sending there."

Mr. Lorry Meets Lucie Manette.

"That gentleman is myself."

"Since the gentleman had already left London, a messenger was sent after him to ask him to please wait for me here in Dover. The bank also told me that the gentleman would give me all the details of the property, some of which would be rather surprising. Naturally, I am eager to know what they are."

"Naturally," agreed Mr. Lorry as he adjusted his wig nervously. Finally he looked directly at the young lady and began his story.

"I will tell you first about one of our bank's customers... a French gentleman of great talents... a scientist... a doctor whom I had the pleasure of serving at Tellson's Bank in Paris at the time of his marriage to an English lady about twenty years ago."

"Then, sir, what you are telling me is my own father's story...." She stopped, her forehead wrinkling in bewilderment. Then a faint smile crossed her face as she went on. "It is a story you know because it was you who

16

Nervous Over the Story He Has To Tell

brought me to England when my mother died, just two years after my father's death."

Mr. Lorry took Lucie's hand and brought it gently to his lips. "Yes, child, it *was* I," he said. "I had a close business relationship with your father, and although I usually keep all personal feelings out of my business —"

Mr. Lorry nervously adjusted his wig again, sighed, then returned to his story. "Yes, this is your father's story. Now, here is the difference. If he had not died when he did, but had rather disappeared, silently and suddenly, sent away to a terrible place by a powerful enemy who could sign some papers imprisoning him for as long as the enemy wished. . . ."

Lucie gasped and grabbed Mr. Lorry's arm.

" . . . If the gentleman's wife had begged the king for news of him and never received a reply . . . and furthermore, if the wife had suffered so much from his disappearance before the birth of her daughter. . . ."

"Yes, yes, what then?" begged Lucie.

"Yes, Yes, What Then?"

" . . . If the mother's suffering was so great that she decided to raise the child to believe that the father was dead. . . . "

Lucie Manette jumped up from her chair and threw herself onto the floor at Mr. Lorry's feet. "I beg you, sir, tell me everything!" she cried, gripping his wrists.

"Please control yourself, Miss Manette!"

And gently lifting her from the floor, Mr. Lorry went on. "Although your mother never stopped searching for your father, she died brokenhearted when you were only two years old. Your parents had no great wealth, and we have found no new money or property, but — "

"But what?" gasped Lucie, tightening her grip on his wrists.

Mr. Lorry took a deep breath. "Your father has been found! Alexandre Manette is alive, but he has changed so much that no one would recognize him. He has been freed from that French prison and taken to the house of a faithful servant in Paris. We are going there

"I Beg You, Sir, Tell Me Everything!"

tomorrow — I, to identify him if I can; you, to comfort him and restore him to health."

The young woman trembled violently. "I will see his ghost, not him!" she whispered as if in a trance. "His ghost has never haunted me! To see him now... never having seen him before... and knowing he is my father, a broken man —"

"There is one more thing you should know," interrupted Mr. Lorry. "He was found under another name. Do not ask any questions about that, for it could be very dangerous in France. The people who put your father in prison still rule the country, and even I, an Englishman and a representative of an important bank, do not dare speak of it or carry papers referring to it. I simply use the code words 'RECALLED TO LIFE' to refer to Alexandre Manette's release from prison."

Lucie Manette did not answer. Sitting perfectly still and silent, her eyes frozen wide open, she had fainted!

Found Under Another Name

Afraid to move, for Lucie's hand was still gripping his, Jarvis Lorry shouted for help. A wild-looking woman with red hair rushed in from an adjoining room. Grabbing Mr. Lorry's jacket with a brawny hand, she lifted him from his chair and sent him flying across the room. Just then, the inn's servants appeared, also in response to the call for help, and the woman sent them scurrying for cold water and smelling salts.

After carrying Lucie to a sofa and stroking her head tenderly, the woman turned to Jarvis Lorry. "Why couldn't you tell her what you had to without frightening her to death?" she shouted. This, then, was Miss Pross, who had taken care of Lucie since childhood and was traveling with her from London to Paris.

Jarvis Lorry could not help feeling ashamed, and after seeing Lucie regain consciousness, he hurridly left the room.

Sent Flying Across the Room!

A Wine Cask Drops from a Cart.

CHAPTER 2

Recalled to Life

Saint Antoine was a poor section of Paris with houses so run-down that the people spent most of their time on the street. Saint Antoine was also filled with hunger, and because of it, the ragged people were filled with hatred toward the wealthy and noble classes of Paris, who cared nothing for their misery. And so it was that Saint Antoine was rapidly becoming a center of unrest — unrest which would soon explode in the French Revolution.

It was in a narrow Saint Antoine street one day that a large cask of wine dropped from a cart and shattered on the rough stones outside a wine shop. All the people on the street stopped what they were doing to run over and drink the wine. Some knelt down, scooped their hands together, and sipped every drop they could find. Others licked the wine from the stones. Mothers dipped rags into the wine and squeezed drops into infants' mouths. Children built little mud walls to trap puddles of wine and drank mixtures of wine and mud.

The wine stains left the street looking blood-stained. And, indeed, it wouldn't be long before blood *would* flow in these very streets!

The owner of the wine shop, a fierce-looking, dark-haired man of about thirty, stood watching the mad scramblings on the street. "It is not my problem," muttered Ernest Defarge with a shrug. "Let the people from the market bring another cask. It's their fault." And with that, he turned and went into his shop.

Therese Defarge, his wife, looked up from her seat behind the counter in the wine shop when her husband entered. Although her

Watching Hungry Peasants Lick Up the Wine

hands were busy knitting, a lift of her eyebrows and a slight nod of her head indicated to her husband that he should notice the elderly gentleman and the young lady seated at a corner table sipping some wine.

Jarvis Lorry and Lucie Manette had also noticed Ernest Defarge when he entered the shop, and with a nod of his head, Mr. Lorry told Lucie, "This is our man."

Monsieur Defarge pretended not to notice the elderly gentleman and the young lady as he went behind the counter to serve a customer.

Madame Defarge coughed and raised her eyebrows even higher, never losing a stitch in her knitting.

As soon as the customer had left the shop, Mr. Lorry went up to the counter and spoke softly with Monsieur Defarge. After they had exchanged a few whispered words, Defarge nodded and headed for the door. Mr. Lorry beckoned to Lucie to follow them out of the

Indicating the Gentleman and Young Lady

shop. Although Madame Defarge continued to knit, her eyes followed her husband and his two visitors out the door.

Defarge led Mr. Lorry and Lucie toward a narrow, winding, tiled staircase off a garbage-filled dark courtyard, which was surrounded by high, rotting buildings.

"Is he alone?" whispered Mr. Lorry.

"Of course. He is always alone," snapped Defarge. "And he is in the same exact state he was in when his friends asked if I would risk taking him in and not breathe a word about the matter to anyone."

They climbed the stairs, and when they reached the closed door at the top, Defarge inserted a key in the lock.

Mr. Lorry turned to Lucie. "Come, child, we are going in to see your father," he said, putting his arm around her waist to support her.

"I'm afraid to see him!" she cried, her knees weakening. "I'm afraid to see my father!

"We Are Going In To See Your Father."

"I See You Are Still Working Hard."

CHAPTER 3

The Shoemaker

The attic was small and dark. A white-haired man was sitting on a low bench, his back to the door, facing the room's only window. He was stooped over a pair of shoes that he was making.

"Good day!" said Monsieur Defarge, walking towards the window. "I see you are still working hard."

The white head was raised for a moment, but did not turn toward the doorway. "Yes, I am working," said a weak, pitiful voice.

An unfinished shoe was in the old man's hand, and some simple tools and scraps of leather were on the bench before him.

"You have a visitor," said Defarge, pointing to Mr. Lorry, who now joined him at the window, leaving Lucie by the door, still out of the shoemaker's sight.

The shoemaker turned and stared blankly at Mr. Lorry. The old man's bright eyes stood out in his hollow face, and his ragged white hair and beard contrasted sharply with his dark eyebrows. His shirt, yellowed with age, was in rags. The hand that he raised to shield his eyes from the light coming through the door was as withered and worn as the rest of his body.

"Tell the gentleman what kind of shoe you are working on," prodded Defarge.

After a long pause, the old man replied, "It is a lady's shoe. A young lady's walking shoe."

"And what is the shoemaker's name?"

"My name? . . . One hundred and five, North Tower." And that was all the old shoemaker said. Then he bent over his work once more.

"My Name?"

"Dr. Manette, don't you remember me?" asked Mr. Lorry, breaking the silence.

The shoemaker turned again and stared at the visitor, the half-finished shoe falling to the floor.

"Don't you remember this man either?" asked Mr. Lorry, pointing to Defarge. "I was your banker, and he was your trusted servant. Don't you remember that?"

The old man stared blankly in turn at Mr. Lorry and Monsieur Defarge. A glimmer appeared in his eyes, then they clouded over again. With a deep sigh, he went back to his shoemaking.

Meanwhile, Lucie had crept along the wall until she could fully see the shoemaker. Her first fears had given way to sorrow and pity... and love. She moved softly to her father's side.

Dr. Manette, not seeing her, put down the tool in his hand and picked up his shoemaker's knife. As he did so, he caught sight of Lucie's

"Don't You Remember This Man?"

skirt. He raised his head slowly until he was looking into her face. Mr. Lorry and Monsieur Defarge took a step forward as if to protect Lucie from the knife in the old man's hand, but she motioned them away.

"What is this?" the shoemaker gasped in a voice that could be scarcely heard.

Without answering, Lucie put her hands to her lips and kissed them to him. Tears streamed down her face.

"You are not the jailer's daughter?" asked the old shoemaker.

"No," whispered Lucie.

"Then who are you?" he gasped weakly.

Lucie could not trust herself to speak yet, but she sat down next to him on the bench and laid her hand on his arm.

A shiver went through the old man's thin frame and he drew back. But then he put the knife down and slowly lifted a few strands of the girl's long golden hair and held it gently between his bony fingers. Then, dropping the hair just as

Lifting the Long Golden Hair

gently against Lucie's slim shoulder, he untied a piece of folded rag from around his neck and opened it carefully. Inside were several strands of long golden hair.

Picking up Lucie's hair again and looking at it closely, the old man gasped, "It is the same! How can it be? When was it?"

Then he gently turned the girl's face fully toward the light, and the words came out. "I remember it very well — that night long ago, when I was called out of the house. She had laid her head on my shoulder. She was afraid for me to go. Then, when I was brought to my prison cell in the North Tower, they found these strands of hair on my sleeve where my daughter had laid her head. The jailer let me keep them, for surely they could not help me escape. But whose hair was it? Was it yours? . . . No, no, it cannot be. . . . Tell me, what is your name, gentle angel?"

Grateful for his softened tone, Lucie fell to her knees before him and reached her arms out

"It Is the Same! How Can It Be?"

toward him, cradling his cold white head among her warm, shining curls. "Oh, dear sir," she whispered through her tears, "you will learn my name at another time. All I can tell you now is that your misery is ended. I will take you to England and make you well and make a home for us!"

The sight of the pitiful man, sunk in his daughter's arms, so touched Lorry and Defarge that they looked away, fearful that unmanly tears would reach their own eyes as well.

Soon after, the two men left to make all the travel arrangements. Lucie stayed with her father, cradling his limp form in her arms.

When all the preparations had been made, Mr. Lorry and Monsieur Defarge returned with hot food and warm traveling cloaks. His face blank with confusion and wonder, Dr. Manette ate and drank as he was told, and allowed Lucie to wrap him in the cloak. He had been confined in prison and in the attic room for so long that he was barely able to walk.

Lucie Wraps Dr. Manette in the Cloak.

As Mr. Lorry helped him down the stairs, Dr. Manette steadfastly clung to Lucie's hand. Monsieur Defarge picked up the shoemaker's bench and tools and followed them down into the street.

Reaching the courtyard, Dr. Manette looked around, searching for the towers of the prison and the guards at their posts. But only one lone figure was in view — Madame Defarge, who leaned against the door of the wine shop, knitting by the light of the lamp post.

The horses and carriage were waiting. Dr. Manette, Lucie, and Mr. Lorry climbed inside.

As the carriage pulled away, Defarge stood looking after it. "I hope he won't regret being 'RECALLED TO LIFE,'" he whispered into the night.

Climbing into the Carriage

The Doctor Returns To Practicing Medicine.

CHAPTER 4

The Trial of Charles Darnay

Five years had passed. It was 1780. Dr. Manette and his daughter lived in a comfortable house in London. The doctor had regained his health and returned to practicing medicine. Mr. Lorry still worked for Tellson's Bank and continued to travel between its London and Paris offices.

England had been at war with her American colonies for five years, but was losing battle after battle. France had come to the aid of the colonists, an act which angered England.

It was because of these bitter feelings that a trial for treason was in progress at the Old

Bailey Courthouse in London. The accused, Charles Darnay, was charged with passing government secrets to the French king about the troops England was sending to North America during the Revolution.

The man standing quietly but confidently in the prisoner's box was a tall, handsome, dark-haired gentleman of about twenty-five. From time to time, Charles Darnay's eyes were drawn to two witnesses sitting in the court-room. They were Dr. Alexandre Manette and his daughter Lucie, whom Charles had met during their trip to England five years before, when Lucie was taking her poor, ill father out of France. Because of this meeting, they were being called to testify against the prisoner, as was Mr. Jarvis Lorry, who had accompanied them on that trip.

The solicitor, or attorney for the British Government, told the jury that he planned to prove that Darnay's treason had started five years ago, on the eve of the Revolution.

At Charles Darnay's Trial

The prisoner's lawyers, Mr. Stryver and Mr. Carton, sat at a long table, Stryver listening intently to the government's solicitor and Carton staring fixedly at the ceiling.

The first witness to be called by the solicitor was Mr. John Barsad, a gentleman and former friend of Charles Darnay.

"Why are you testifying against the prisoner?" began the solicitor.

"Because I discovered his traitorous schemes, sir, and being a patriot, I reported them to the government immediately."

"And what were these traitorous schemes?"

"He was supplying the French with lists, in his very own handwriting, of British troop movements to the colonies."

When it was Mr. Stryver's turn to cross examine Barsad, he showed that far from being a gentleman, Barsad was an ex-convict and a gambler, and far from being Darnay's friend, had only met him once, in a coach.

The solicitor then called Roger Cly, Darnay's

The Prisoner's Lawyers

servant, as the next witness. "How long have you worked for the prisoner?" began the solicitor.

"About four years," replied Cly.

"Have you ever seen the prisoner with papers listing the troops and military equipment that England was sending to North America?"

"Yes, I did."

"Where?"

"In Mr. Darnay's pockets and in his desk."

"And did you ever see him give those papers to anyone else?"

"Yes, to some French gentleman on the boat that travels between Dover and Calais."

"What do you expect to gain by giving this evidence against the prisoner?"

"Nothing whatsoever. I am doing it for the love of my country. I am a true Englishman."

Under cross-examination by Stryver, Cly admitted to having been a thief and working at one time for the French Government.

Roger Cly Is Questioned.

The solicitor next called Mr. Jarvis Lorry to the witness stand. "Think back five years, Mr. Lorry, to a certain Friday night in November, 1775," he began. "Were you then traveling on business from London to Dover by mail coach?"

"I was," replied the banker.

"Were there any other passengers in the coach?"

"Yes, two men."

"Did those two men leave the coach in the middle of the night and continue on the road by foot?"

"They did."

"Was the prisoner, Charles Darnay, one of them?"

"I really don't know, sir," replied Mr. Lorry, looking at Darnay. "They were so covered up and the night was so dark that I couldn't really see them well enough to identify them."

"Have you ever seen the prisoner before, Mr. Lorry?"

Mr. Lorry Recalls a Night in 1775.

"Yes, when I was returning from France a few days after that. Mr. Darnay was on the same boat that brought me back to England."

"At what time did he come aboard at Calais?"

"A little after midnight."

"Were you traveling alone, Mr. Lorry?"

"No, sir. I was with two companions, Dr. Alexandre Manette and his daughter Lucie."

"And did you speak to the prisoner during that trip?"

"No, it was a stormy night and I spent the entire trip in my cabin."

"Thank you, Mr. Lorry," said the solicitor. "That will be all. You may step down. I now call upon Miss Lucie Manette to testify."

The young lady approached the witness stand slowly, looking with great pity at Charles Darnay.

"Miss Manette, when did you first meet the prisoner?" asked the solicitor.

"On the boat Mr. Lorry just referred to. I

Lucie Looks at Charles with Pity.

had made a bed for my father on the deck because he was very tired and weak, and I wanted to give him some fresh air. Mr. Darnay came over and suggested how I could better protect my father from the wind and cold. He was very kind and gentle toward my father and I was most grateful to him."

"Did the prisoner come on the boat alone?"

"No, sir, he was with two French gentlemen who got off the boat before it left Calais."

"What were they doing while on board?"

"They were looking at some papers and whispering."

"What kind of papers were they looking at?"

"I don't know."

"Did the prisoner mention to you anything about his business?"

Lucie looked at Charles Darnay and started to sob. Then, turning back to the solicitor, said, "Mr. Darnay was so kind to my father that I hope I won't do him any harm today."

"He Was with Two French Gentlemen."

"This is your duty, Miss Manette!" snapped the judge. "Just tell the jury what he said!"

"He told me that he was traveling on important business — business that could get some people into trouble. Because of that, he was traveling under the false name of Charles Darnay. He also said that this business would be taking him back and forth between England and France for a long time to come."

"Did he say whether or not that business concerned the American colonies?"

"He said England was foolish to quarrel with America. He even said jokingly that George Washington might become as famous in history as King George the Third!"

This answer brought a buzz in the courtroom and a glare from the judge as he made his notes. "An insult to our King!" he thought.

"Thank you, Miss Manette," said the solicitor when all was quiet again. "That will be all. I now call Dr. Alexandre Manette to testify."

Clearing his throat, the solicitor began. "Do

"Just Tell the Jury What He Said!"

you remember the prisoner as the same man you met on the boat five years ago?"

"I cannot recall, sir. I do not remember anything about that period," said the doctor.

"Dr. Manette, did you spend a long time in prison in France without a trial?"

"A long time, sir. And because of it, my mind is a blank — or it was until I found myself one day in my London home with my dear daughter caring for me."

"Thank you, Dr. Manette. I have no more questions," said the solicitor.

The doctor left the witness box and went to rejoin his daughter. As they sat down, a new witness was called.

Under questioning, the man testified that on that Friday night in 1775, he had seen the prisoner waiting for someone in a hotel in a town near where the two passengers had left the mail coach. The solicitor tried to convince the jury that Darnay had left the coach in the dead of night and walked to the hotel to

"My Mind Is Blank."

exchange secret military information.

Then Charles Darnay's attorney, Mr. Stryver, began to cross-examine the witness. Just then, Mr. Stryver's associate, Mr. Carton, who had not taken any part in the proceedings up to that point, lowered his head from its fixed stare at the ceiling, removed his attorney's wig, and wrote something on a piece of paper.

Although Carton himself had a brilliant mind, his laziness and constant drinking prevented him from becoming a success on his own. Therefore, he had to be content with working for Mr. Stryver, whose successful law practice made Carton extremely jealous.

Carton folded the note and passed it to Stryver, who upon reading it, immediately turned back to the witness he was questioning.

"Are you absolutely certain that the man in the hotel was the prisoner Charles Darnay?"

"I am quite sure."

"Did you ever see anyone who looks very

Carton Passes a Note to Stryver.

much like the prisoner?"

"Not so much alike that I could mistake the two."

"Look, then, at that man over there!" ordered Stryver, pointing to Sidney Carton. "Then look back at the prisoner!"

The two men looked so much alike that they surprised not only each other, but the judge, the witness, and the entire courtroom as well!

Mr. Stryver then summed up his case for the defense. He maintained that John Barsad was a liar, Roger Cly a hired spy and traitor, and that the final witness could not really identify the prisoner as the man he had seen at the hotel.

The jury then left the room to decide the prisoner's fate.

Afternoon stretched into the evening. Lamps were lit in the courtroom. The spectators brought in mutton pies and ale for refreshment. Finally, the jury returned with the verdict — NOT GUILTY!

Ordering the Witness to Look at Two Men

The crowds in the courtroom spilled out the doors, and Charles Darnay found himself standing face to face with Sidney Carton.

"Here are two look-alikes, that fate has thrown together," said Carton with a drunken laugh.

"Then is it fate that also makes me feel faint?" asked Darnay.

"Hardly!" replied Carton. "It is hunger. Come, let us dine together."

Once the two men were seated in a nearby tavern, with food and wine restoring Darnay's strength, he thanked Carton warmly.

"You don't have to thank me," said the attorney after a long gulp of wine. "It was nothing. But it must feel good to have such a beautiful young lady as Lucie Manette pity you and cry for you."

Carton drank as Charles ate, and continued drinking long after dinner was finished. Finally, Charles rose to go.

"If you want to know why I am getting

Fate Has Thrown Two Look-Alikes Together.

drunk," Carton called after him, "it is because I am disappointed with life. I am a failure at everything — my work, my friends.... You are everything I am not. No blue eyes would fill with tears for me, as Lucie Manette's did for you. But no matter! I care for no man, and no man cares for me!"

"I'm sorry to hear that," Darnay replied to the figure now slumped over the emptied wine bottles. "You might have made better use of your brilliant talents."

Later that evening, wakening from a drunken sleep at the tavern, Sidney Carton went to Mr. Stryver's office to help with some legal papers, a practice the two followed daily. While Stryver was a popular and successful attorney, the truth was that his brilliance in the courtroom came about as a result of his evenings' work with Carton, whose shrewd mind solved many of Stryver's cases.

"You were brilliant today, Sidney," said Stryver as the two seated themselves at a

"I Am a Failure at Everything."

table covered with piles of papers and bottles of wine. "What gave you that idea of the look-alikes?"

"I just thought that Darnay was a handsome fellow and that I might have been like him if I had had some luck."

"No, it's not luck, my friend. It's hard work and helping yourself — something you never even try. You are content to help others, but never yourself. You were that way when we were at law school too. Why is that?"

"Who knows? But let's not talk about that."

"Very well then. Shall we talk about that pretty young witness?"

"I don't think she's that pretty."

"You are protesting too much, Sidney."

And to that, Sidney Carton had no answer. He was feeling very sorry for himself and had drunk too much as usual, so he decided to go home to bed, where he shed his tears of frustration and unhappiness on a pillow that had felt countless nights of tears.

"You Help Others, But Never Yourself."

Terrible Reminders of Years in Prison

CHAPTER 5

A Moment of Terror

Four months had passed since Charles Darnay's trial. It was a Sunday afternoon and Jarvis Lorry had come to call on the Manettes in their small house in London. While waiting in the doctor's room for his hosts to appear, Mr. Lorry's eyes fixed on the shoemaker's bench and tools—those terrible reminders of Dr. Manette's years in prison.

"What are you staring at?" demanded a voice behind him.

Mr. Lorry turned at the sound of Miss Pross' voice, remembering his first meeting with this wild-eyed woman in Dover five years ago. Knowing of her devotion to Lucie and the doctor, he explained, "I was just wondering why the doctor still keeps those things."

"I wouldn't know," snapped Miss Pross. "But I do know that we are having more visitors today — another of these young men who are unworthy of my dear Lucie's time. Only one man could ever be worthy of her — my dear brother Solomon . . . if only he hadn't made that one mistake in life."

Mr. Lorry knew that the one "mistake" made by Solomon Pross was taking all of his sister's belongings years ago and leaving her in poverty. But that did not concern him now.

Just then, Dr. Manette and Lucie entered the room, and they all went out into the garden. They were sitting there, talking of old buildings in London, when Charles Darnay arrived.

Joining in their discussion, Charles asked, "Have any of you seen much of the Tower? I was imprisoned there before my trial."

Talking in the Garden

"Lucie and I have been there a few times," answered the doctor. "It's quite interesting."

"Well, when I was there, I learned something very curious. It seems that while some repairs were being made, workmen came across an old dungeon that hadn't been used for many years. Every stone of its inner wall was covered with names, dates and complaints written by the prisoners. While digging under the floor, the workmen found the ashes of a paper. Some unknown prisoner had written a note and hidden it from the jailer. What was written will never be known."

Dr. Manette gasped, and his hands flew up to his head. Terror spread across his face for a moment.

"Are you ill, Father?" cried Lucie.

"No, dear," said the doctor, recovering himself quickly. "I just felt some raindrops. We should go inside."

But Mr. Lorry had seen that look of terror, and it sent a shudder through him.

Terror on Dr. Manette's Face!

The Marquis Is Ignored by the King.

CHAPTER 6

The Marquis St. Evremonde

The Marquis St. Evremonde, a nobleman at the king's court in France, had attended a fancy reception at the palace one day in 1780. The expensive clothes and jewelry worn by the guests and the delicious feast spread on the table contrasted sharply with the rags and the empty stomachs of the masses of people who lived within a short ride of the palace.

When the reception was over, the Marquis, a haughty, handsomely dressed man of about sixty, climbed into his coach, anxious to leave Paris as quickly as possible. He had been ignored by the king at the reception, and his anger was still with him. So, he rather enjoyed the reckless speed with which his driver was handling his coach, for it made the common people scatter before him.

As the coach swooped around one corner, a sickening thud was heard. The horses reared, and loud cries reached the Marquis' ears. He would have ordered the driver to proceed, had not twenty hands grabbed the horses' reins. Leaning out the window, he saw a tall man in a nightcap picking up a bundle from under the horses' hoofs. The man knelt down in the mud and began howling like a wild animal.

"Pardon, Monsieur the Marquis!" said a ragged man, "but it is his child."

When the man rose and rushed toward the carriage, the Marquis reached for his sword.

"Killed!" screamed the father. "Dead!"

The Marquis looked out at the crowd and reached for his purse. " I can't understand why you people can't take care of yourselves and your children!" he said. "One of you is always

"It Is His Child."

in the way of the coach. To think that you might have injured my horses! Here, give the man this!"

He tossed a gold coin down into the street. At that moment, a man rushed over to the sobbing father and comforted him. "Be brave, Gaspar! It is better for the poor child to die without pain than to live with the pain of hunger and such injuries."

"You are a wise man," said the Marquis, smiling. "What is your name?"

"I am Defarge, the wine seller."

"Pick that up and spend it as you will," said the Marquis, tossing another gold coin out of the carriage. But as he sat back in his seat with a satisfied smile, the coin came flying back into the carriage.

"Who threw that?" shouted the Marquis.

He looked at the spot where Defarge had been standing. The poor father lay sobbing on the pavement, and beside him stood a dark-haired woman knitting.

"Be Brave, Gaspard!"

Getting no reply from the silent peasants — only a long, hard stare from Madame Defarge — the Marquis ordered his carriage on.

Hours later, the carriage entered a poor village at sunset and stopped at a posting house — a stable — to change horses. Many poor peasants gathered around the coach, including a grizzled man in a blue cap.

"Monsieur the Marquis," said the man, removing his cap as he approached. "I am a road fixer. As your carriage was coming along the road outside the village, I saw a man swinging by the chain underneath it!"

"Who was he?" snapped the Marquis, who hated to waste time talking with people of the lower classes.

"He wasn't from this part of the country. I never saw him before in my life, Monsieur!"

"What did he look like?"

"Your carriage was traveling too quickly for me to get a good look, Monsieur."

The Marquis sent for Monsieur Gabelle, who

"I Saw a Man Swinging by the Chain."

was in charge of the posting house and who thus knew whenever a stranger entered the village.

"Get your hands on this stranger if he tries to spend the night in this village!" ordered the Marquis. Then to his driver, he shouted, "Be off!"

The coach drove off at great speed, and later that evening the Marquis arrived at his castle to keep an appointment with his nephew Charles, who was arriving from England.

When the two were seated over dinner, the Marquis asked Charles Darnay why he had returned to France.

"Sir," said Charles, "ours is an honorable family, but we have mistreated the people and now we are paying for it. My father punished everyone who interfered with his pleasures, and you, my father's twin brother and heir to his property, have also done wrong. My mother, on her deathbed, begged me to be merciful to the people and to make up for the wrongs you both have

Orders to Gabelle

done. I have been trying to do this for years and have returned to France to continue to help the poor peasants."

"We were born into this family," said the Marquis sternly, "and I, for one, will fight to keep these revolutionary peasants from changing the ruling system in France, even if it means fighting and imprisoning you as well!"

"This property and my country are both lost to me," Charles answered sadly. "France is a land of misery and ruin. I will live somewhere else and work to support myself."

"Hah!" cried the Marquis, looking around the luxurious room. "You will live in England, I suppose?"

"Yes. There I will not feel ashamed of my family name, for I do not use it."

"Other Frenchmen have fled to England. Do you know a doctor and his daughter?" the Marquis asked with a sly smile.

"Yes, I do. Why do you ask?"

Without replying to his nephew, the Marquis

The Marquis Warns Charles.

ended the conversation by calling a servant and ordering him to show Charles to his room. Then the Marquis went to his own bed chamber.

As he lay in bed waiting for sleep to come, he thought about the day that had passed: the palace reception, the child killed by the carriage, the grieving father, the fixer of roads, and the tale of the man hanging from the coach. "A very bad day, indeed," he muttered as sleep finally came.

As the Marquis slept, the stone faces on the castle's front walls stared out into the black night, sounding no alarm as silent footsteps crept toward the gates.

When the sun rose the following morning, there was another stone face at the castle — that of the Marquis on his pillow. A mask of fear was frozen on his face and a knife lay driven into his heart. Around the handle was a note: HE IS READY FOR HIS TOMB. FROM JACQUES.

Stone Faces Outside *and* Inside the Castle

Charles Asks For Lucie's Hand

CHAPTER 7

Sidney's Confession

During the following year, Charles Darnay became a popular and successful teacher and translator of French. As his success grew, so did his love for Lucie Manette. And so it was, one summer day, that he decided to ask Dr. Manette for Lucie's hand in marriage.

"I know that you love her," said the doctor. "But does Lucie know of your love, of your wish to marry her?"

"No, sir. I thought it proper to speak to you first, in case there were other suitors."

"Well, Mr. Carton calls on us often."

"There is something else, sir," said Charles.

"I do not wish there to be any secrets between us. I wish to tell you my real name and why I am living in England."

"Stop!" cried the doctor, placing his fingers over Charles' lips. "Do not tell me now! If you and Lucie marry, you can tell me on your wedding day. Now go, before Lucie returns. I must speak to her alone."

When Lucie came home an hour later, she was surprised to find her father's reading chair empty. Then, a sudden hammering sound came from Dr. Manette's bedroom. Lucie froze with fear, realizing that her father was working at his shoemaker's bench. Trembling, she ran upstairs and gently helped him to his feet. She walked with him back and forth for many hours, and it was late at night when she finally left him sleeping peacefully.

During that same year, another man also fell in love with Lucie Manette, but unlike Charles Darnay, Sidney Carton did not feel himself worthy of her. He had not made a suc-

Lucie Freezes with Fear!

cess of his life and he drank too much, yet something in him drove him to confide his feelings to Lucie anyhow. So it was that one afternoon, Sidney's feet carried him to the neat Manette house.

When Lucie received him in her sitting-room, she noticed a rather strange look on his face. "Are you ill, Mr. Carton?" she asked.

"No, but the life I lead is rather unhealthy."

"Forgive me for asking, but wouldn't it be better to change your way of life?"

"It is too late to change," he said, as tears filled his eyes. "I shall never be any better than I am now, and I fear that I shall sink even lower. However, I do hope that you will listen to what I have to say."

"If it will make you feel better, of course I will listen!"

"Thank you for your kindness, Miss Manette. If you were able to return the love of the man you see here before you — this drunken, wasted, good-for-nothing man — he

Sidney Confides His Feelings to Lucie.

could bring you only misery. And so I am thankful that our love can never be."

"But can I not help you, Mr. Carton, in some other way?"

"No, Miss Manette. I am grateful just to have you listen to me. I didn't think I had any feelings for home and family left until I saw your beautiful face and the lovely home you have made for yourself and your father."

"But could I not influence you to change your life for the better, Mr. Carton?"

"You have influenced me, Miss Manette, to open my heart to you as I have not done to anyone else. And I beg you never tell anyone what I have confided to you."

"I promise."

"Thank you," he said. And he lifted her hand to his lips. "Please always remember and believe that the true Sidney Carton is the man here with you now, the man who would lay down his life for you. . . . Farewell, my dear Miss Manette, and God bless you!"

A Promise To Lay Down His Life for Her

"It's a Funeral Procession."

CHAPTER 8

The Grave Robbers

Jerry Cruncher, the messenger, was sitting outside Tellson's Bank as usual, when a mob came marching down Fleet Street.

"It's a funeral procession," he told his son, who was sitting beside him.

Jerry was always attracted by funerals, but this one was very unusual, for people were running alongside the carriage that held the coffin, shouting, "Spies! Spies!"

When someone whispered that the dead man was a Roger Cly, Jerry muttered to himself, "The man at Charles Darnay's trial!"

Jerry followed the mob to the graveyard,

watched the burial, and then went home. That night, he told his wife and son that he was going fishing.

"But how come whenever you fish at night, your boots get so dirty and you get rust under your fingernails?" asked his son.

"No more questions! It's time for bed!" snapped Jerry.

When his family was asleep (or so he believed), Jerry unlocked a cabinet and took out a sack, a crowbar, a rope, and a chain.

His son slipped out of bed and followed his father at a safe distance. Two more "fishermen" appeared, and the three men walked quickly along a lonely road. Then they climbed over an iron gate.

Peering through the gate, the boy saw the men "fishing" among the graves in the churchyard. When they raised a coffin to the surface, the boy ran home terrified!

There was no fish for breakfast the following morning at the Cruncher house.

"Fishing" Among the Graves!

"He Is a Fixer of Roads."

CHAPTER 9

Spies

Madame Defarge sat in the wine shop, her fingers knitting but her eyes on the look-out for spies that were always being sent into the Saint Antoine section by the king.

"Good day, my wife!" called Ernest Defarge, returning from a three-day trip to the country. "On my journey, I met this good gentleman." And he pointed to a man with a blue cap beside him. "He is a fixer of roads. Give my new friend some breakfast!"

When the two men had finished their morning meal and the shop was emptied of all customers except two, Defarge and the road fixer joined them at their table.

"Now that all of our good 'Jacques' are here, we may begin," said Defarge, using the code name "Jacques" that the revolutionaries used to identify each other. "I shall be Jacques One, and here —" and he pointed to the road fixer, "— here is Jacques Two. Speak, Jacques Two, and tell them everything."

"It was a year ago this summer," began the road fixer, taking off his blue cap, "when I first saw Gaspard. He was hanging by a chain under the Marquis' carriage. But I had no idea that he was planning to kill him."

"When did you see him again?" asked Jacques Three.

"Well, Gaspard ran away after he killed the Marquis and managed to avoid the soldiers for months and months. But he was finally caught, and when I next saw him, he was hanging from a gallows forty feet high in the village square. I was so enraged at this that I left the village at sunset and walked all that

The Road Fixer Tells His Story.

night and half the next day until I met
Jacques." And he pointed at Defarge.

"You are a good man!" said Defarge. "And
worthy of joining our cause. But please leave
the shop for a moment, as we must talk."

After the road fixer had gone out the door,
Jacques Three turned to the other men.
"What do you say, Jacques?" he asked Defarge.
"Do we put the village officials on our list?"

"To be listed as doomed for destruction!"
replied Defarge.

"Are you sure that problems won't arise as a
result of our keeping this list of our enemies'
names?" asked Jacques Four. "I know it is safe,
because no one besides us, or rather *she,* can
understand it."

"Don't worry," answered Defarge. "Even if
my wife kept the list in her head, she would
never forget it. But the list is knitted in a
special pattern and design so that it will
always be plain as day to her. There is no way
that a single letter of an enemy's name or a

"The List Is Knitted in a Special Design."

single crime can be erased from Madame Defarge's knitted list!"

After the fixer of roads was sent back to his village to spy for his new friends, Defarge learned from one of his "Jacques" on the police force that a new spy was being sent to Saint Antoine. He informed his wife of this immediately.

"He will be put on my list as soon as I see him!" she said. "What is his name?"

"John Barsad. An Englishman."

The very next day, that Englishman entered the wine shop. Madame Defarge was knitting as usual.

"You knit very well, Madame!" said Barsad, after ordering some wine. "And an interesting design too. What are you making?"

"Nothing special. I knit just to keep busy." And her fingers knitted J-O-H-N into the design.

"Business seems bad," commented the spy.

"It is very bad," said Madame Defarge.

"You Knit Very Well, Madame!"

"The people are so poor." And the name B-A-R-S-A-D was knitted into the list.

"These miserable people are badly treated too, isn't that so?"

"If you say so."

"You don't agree?"

"My husband and I have enough to do just to run this wine shop. We have no time to think of other people."

This conversation was getting the spy nowhere! He tried another subject. "It's too bad about poor Gaspard," he said with a great sigh. "To be executed that way."

"I'm sure he knew that if he killed someone, he in turn would be executed," said Madame.

"I believe," said the spy, dropping his voice, "that there is much pity and anger around here about Gaspard. Don't you think so?"

"Here is my husband!" said Madame Defarge, ignoring the question.

"Good day, Jacques!" said the spy, tipping his hat.

The Spy Greets Monsieur Defarge.

"You are mistaken, sir. That is not my name; I am Ernest Defarge."

"Well, no matter! While talking with your wife, I remembered some interesting things connected with your name."

"Oh?"

"Yes, when Dr. Alexandre Manette was freed, he was brought to you, his old house servant."

"That is true," said Defarge, whose wife gave him a look that said to answer the spy in as few words as possible.

"His daughter also came to you," Barsad continued. "She was with a gentleman from Tellson's Bank."

"That is true," repeated Defarge.

"You don't hear from them anymore?"

"No," broke in Madame. "We got a letter saying that they had arrived safely in England and then another letter, but not any more."

"The girl is going to be married," said Barsad. "Married to a Frenchman by birth. In

Barsad Tries To Get Information.

fact, her husband-to-be is a nephew of the Marquis that Gaspard killed. In England, he goes under the name of Charles Darnay."

Madame Defarge kept knitting, but the news had a strong effect on her husband, who trembled visibly as he lit his pipe.

Having finally gotten some reaction, however small, from his day's work, the spy paid for his wine and left the shop.

"Can what he just said about Lucie's marriage be true?" Defarge whispered to his wife.

"What if it is?" she asked calmly.

" . . . Well, if the revolution comes during our lifetime, I hope for Lucie Manette's sake that fate keeps her husband out of France!"

"Fate will lead him where he has to go!" snapped Madame Defarge.

"But how strange it is that after we felt so much sympathy for Dr. Manette and Lucie, you are now knitting the name of her husband into your list alongside that spy Barsad!"

The News Has a Strong Effect on Defarge.

Lucie and Charles Are Married.

CHAPTER 10

Sound Medical Advice

Only Dr. Manette, Mr. Lorry, and Miss Pross attended the wedding in the small church. Lucie was a beautiful bride and Charles a handsome groom. Although the doctor appeared happy, Mr. Lorry could not help remembering the deadly fear that covered his face earlier that morning when he emerged from a private meeting with Charles.

After the newlyweds had left for their honeymoon, Mr. Lorry saw that same fear return to the doctor's face. Shortly after the doctor went to his room to rest, Miss Pross heard the sound of hammering.

She rushed inside, then came out immediately.

"All is lost!" she cried to Mr. Lorry. "He doesn't know who I am, and he's gone back to making shoes!"

Mr. Lorry hurried in. The doctor was busy at work and didn't recognize him either.

Nine days passed, and still the shoemaker sat at his bench. For the first time in his life, Jarvis Lorry took time off from Tellson's Bank, to help Miss Pross care for the doctor, to talk to him, and to try to bring his mind back. On the tenth day, however, Mr. Lorry found the shoemaker's bench put aside and the doctor in his reading chair.

Knowing he would have to give a reason for calling on the doctor so early in the day, Mr. Lorry asked, "My dear Dr. Manette, would you kindly give me some medical advice about the case of a good friend of mine who has been acting strangely? For his sake and the sake of his daughter, I beg your help!"

Mr. Lorry, of course, was referring to Dr.

"He's Gone Back To Making Shoes!"

Manette's own strange behavior, but by pretending he was talking about someone else, he hoped to awaken the doctor's mind to what had happened the last nine days.

"Did your friend have some kind of mental shock?" asked the doctor.

"Yes, sir. The shock was due to long years of great suffering. My friend later recovered, but has now experienced a relapse of the shock."

"How long did this relapse last?"

"Nine days and nine nights."

"You mentioned a daughter. Does she know about the relapse?"

"No, it has been kept secret from her."

"That's very thoughtful of you," said the doctor, grasping Mr. Lorry's hand in relief. "I believe your friend expected and feared this relapse," he continued. "I believe something caused your friend to remember the circumstances that led to the first instance of this strange behavior. His daughter, or even someone else, might have said or done something to

Mr. Lorry Discusses a "Friend."

make him remember events that happened before his first period of suffering."

"Do you think the strange behavior might recur again in the future, doctor?"

"I offer your friend hope for the future. His quick recovery this time is a good sign."

"I'm so thankful to hear that, doctor! Now, just one more question. Let us say that during his years of suffering, my friend worked as a blacksmith, making horseshoes and other things out of iron at his forge, and that during the relapse he was found at his forge with his tools again. Should they be taken away?"

"Your friend may have needed to do blacksmith's work to keep him from thinking about his years of suffering," said the doctor nervously. "He may therefore want to keep his blacksmith's tools nearby in case he begins thinking again about that painful period."

"I understand, sir," said Mr. Lorry. "But doesn't keeping the forge and tools make him think all the more about that awful past? If

"I Offer Your Friend Hope."

they were gone, wouldn't his fear go too?"

"The forge and tools, however, are like old friends. . . . " The doctor's voice trailed off.

"I would certainly suggest that my friend get rid of the forge and tools," said Mr. Lorry. "I only want your permission to tell him. Please advise me, for his daughter's sake!"

"In her name, then, let it be done!" said Dr. Manette with a sigh. "But be sure not to take the things away when he is at home."

For the next few days, Mr. Lorry took the doctor for rides in the country, and the old man began to look better and better.

On the fourteenth day, when Dr. Manette was strong enough to go out on his own, Mr. Lorry and Miss Pross went into his room, feeling like criminals. They chopped the shoemaker's bench into little pieces and threw them into the fireplace. Then they buried the tools, shoes, and leather in the garden.

When Lucie and Charles returned to Dr. Manette's house from their honeymoon, their

Destroying the Shoemaker's Bench!

first visitor was Sidney Carton. He had come to apologize to Charles for being rude and drunk on the night after the trial, and to ask permission to visit the family occasionally and be considered their friend.

To this, Charles and Lucie agreed, with Lucie telling her husband after Sidney had gone, "His heart is bleeding, and we must be kind to him. He is capable of gentle things, good things, even great things!"

Time passed, and Lucie gave birth to a baby girl. As the child grew and began to walk and talk, she became the favorite with her "Uncle" Sidney, who visited often, bringing little Lucie gifts and playing with her for hours. He never smelled from wine on these visits!

On a hot night in July, 1789, when little Lucie was six years old, Mr. Lorry came to the house to bring the news to Charles and Lucie and Dr. Manette that the Revolution had broken out in France!

"Uncle" Sidney's Favorite Child

The Defarges Arm the People!

CHAPTER 11

The Revolution Erupts

The people of Saint Antoine were armed. They carried loaded muskets, iron and wooden bars, knives, and axes, and even lifted paving stones from walls and streets. The people were tired of being poor and hungry, and their anger at the king and the noblemen had reached the boiling point.

The center of the raging boil was Defarge's wine shop. Defarge himself, covered with gunpowder and sweat, was issuing orders and giving out weapons.

Madame Defarge's hands no longer held her knitting, but rather an axe and a pistol. In her belt was a knife. "I will lead the women!" she cried. "We can kill as well as men can!"

"We are ready!" shouted Defarge. "Patriots and friends, on to the Bastille!"

With a roar, the mob began to march toward that huge prison, crossing deep ditches, scaling stone walls, and struggling against cannon fire during the two-hour attack.

"The first drawbridge is down!" Defarge shouted. "Work, friends! Work, Jacques Two, Jacques Three, Jacques One Hundred, Jacques One Thousand! Work!"

But there was another drawbridge and also eight high towers. It took four more hours, with guns and torches blazing, before victory was won. A white flag of surrender was raised inside the Bastille, and in another moment, Defarge and the twenty thousand "Jacques" were swept into the outer courtyard of the great stone fortress!

"Free the prisoners!" they cried.

"Seize the records!"

The Attack on the Bastille Begins!

"Find the secret cells!"

"Destroy the instruments of torture!"

Grabbing a prison guard, Defarge demanded, "Show me 105 North Tower! Quick!"

Following the guard up and down mountains of dark stone steps, Defarge, with Jacques Three close behind, reached the cell. The small, dirty room contained a stool, a table, and a straw bed. The walls were black with soot, and a pile of ashes lay on the hearth. There was a single tiny window high up in one of the walls, with a heavy iron bar across it.

"Move your torch slowly along the walls!" Defarge ordered the guard.

"Stop! Look here, Jacques! The letters 'A.M.'! Alexandre Manette! And here the words 'a poor physician.' Quick! Give me your crowbar, Jacques!"

Defarge took the weapon, smashed the table and stool to pieces, then banged against the iron grates across the windows and chimney until they came loose. He also cut the bed

Inside 105 North Tower!

apart with his knife and searched through the straw. Finding nothing, he crawled inside the fireplace and began prying loose the stones with his crowbar and searching the openings with his torch until his hand closed around a packet of papers.

The mob outside the Bastille were grabbing soldiers and guards, beating, shooting and knifing them until they fell dead. Some were strung up on lamp posts; others had their heads chopped off. The streets where the wine cask had once spilled were red again, but this time with blood!

The Bastille was but one place to feel the mob's anger. Prisons and palaces throughout France were attacked and burned. So it was that the darkness above one village was broken by orange flames leaping from a castle on the hill. A road fixer watched smiling as the great stone heads tumbled from its walls, bringing down with them all that remained of the castle of the Marquis St. Evremonde.

Defarge Finds a Packet of Papers.

French Nobles Gather at Tellson's.

CHAPTER 12

Dangerous Journey

It was 1792 — three years later, but still the revolution raged. France no longer had a king and queen, and most of the nobility had fled to England and other countries. A favorite gathering place for the French noblemen was Tellson's Bank in London. As the revolution had neared, many sent their money and jewels to the bank's London office for safekeeping.

At Tellson's office in Paris, which was a city in chaos, there was fear that rampaging mobs would break in and destroy important papers. Someone from the London office had to journey to Paris to see that the bank's papers and records were protected or hidden, for it was nearly impossible to get them out of France.

Jarvis Lorry offered to go.

"I wish I could go in your place," said Charles Darnay to the banker. "The trip is long and difficult, especially in winter. Paris is in great disorder, and you might be in danger."

"Me in danger?" cried Mr. Lorry in surprise. "No, Charles, you would be, for you are French by birth and a nobleman too, and you left your native land to live in England. Imagine how frightened Lucie would be if she ever dreamed that you were thinking of going to Paris!"

"I thought that perhaps I might be able to persuade the revolutionaries to be less violent. . . ."

"Enough, Charles!" interrupted Mr. Lorry. "I am going! I am leaving tonight!"

"Alone?"

"I'm taking Jerry Cruncher with me."

"Me in Danger?"

Just then, a bank clerk approached Mr. Lorry's desk with a letter. As he handed it to the banker, Charles saw the writing on the front:

Urgent! To be forwarded to the Monsieur who used to be known as the Marquis St. Evremonde of France.

Charles paled. No one except Dr. Manette, to whom he had confided his secret on the morning of his wedding, knew his real name. Not Lucie, not Mr. Lorry — no one!

Mr. Lorry looked at the letter, then explained to Charles, "For weeks I have been asking every Frenchman I know, but no one can tell me where this Marquis St. Evremonde can be found."

Charles turned to Mr. Lorry. "I know the fellow," he said quietly. "I will deliver the letter."

Returning home quickly, Charles locked himself in his study and opened the letter. It was from Theophile Gabelle, the keeper of the

A Letter for Mr. Lorry

posting house in the village whose land was owned by the St. Evremonde family. It read:

"Monsieur, formerly the Marquis, Having long been in danger of my life at the hands of the villagers, I have been seized and brought to Paris, to the Prison of the Abbaye. I will have a trial and surely be sentenced to die. My crime is said to be treason against the people, treason because I have served you. They don't listen when I tell them that you were on their side and that you ordered me not to collect rent from them and even to return the taxes they paid to your uncle and to your father. I pray that you will return and save me! I beg you to help me, to be true to me as I have been to you!

Your suffering servant, Gabelle"

Charles made a decision at that moment — he would return to France, not only to save his loyal servant, but to restore his good name as well. But no one would know of his plans, not even Lucie, until he was gone.

That night, Charles sat up late writing two

Reading Gabelle's Plea for Help

letters — one to Lucie and one to her father, explaining the reasons for his journey. By the time the letters were read the following morning, Charles was gone.

The trip to Paris would have been difficult in the best of times. During the French Revolution, however, special dangers lurked. At every village, Charles met citizen-patriots, their muskets raised as they demanded identification papers and checked names against their own lists. It was only by paying for the protection of armed patriots that he finally reached the gates of Paris.

"Where are this prisoner's papers?" a revolutionary guard demanded.

Charles started at the term "prisoner," but produced his papers and Gabelle's letter. Moments later, he was led into a guard-room filled with soldiers and citizens, all wearing the red caps and red, white, and blue feathers of the Revolution.

"Citizen Defarge," said an officer to the

Charles Produces His Papers.

guard, "is this the emigrant Evremonde?"

"Yes."

Turning to Charles, the officer announced, "Evremonde, you have been sentenced to the prison of La Force! "

"Good Heavens!" exclaimed Charles. "Why?"

"We have new laws and new crimes since you left France."

"But I have returned to France of my own free will, in answer to a letter from a fellow Frenchman—a letter that you have just read. Do I not have a right to do that?"

"Emigrants have no rights! Now follow Citizen Defarge!"

Once they were outside, Defarge whispered, "Aren't you the man who married the daughter of Dr. Alexandre Manette, once a prisoner in the Bastille?"

"Yes," answered Charles with surprise.

"My name is Ernest Defarge, and I have a wine shop in Saint Antoine. Maybe you have

"You Have Been Sentenced to Prison!"

heard of me from your —"

"Yes! My wife came to your shop to be reunited with her father!"

"Why on earth did you come back to France?" asked Defarge.

"You heard me tell your officer why I am here. Don't you believe me?"

"It's not important whether I do or not."

"Then, please answer just one question for me — will I be left to rot unjustly in the prison without being able to communicate with the outside world?"

"Who knows? Many other people have been put in prison unjustly too."

"But please, Citizen Defarge, it is of the greatest importance that I tell Mr. Lorry of Tellson's Bank, an English gentleman who is now in Paris, that I have been thrown into La Force. Can you arrange for that message to be delivered?"

"I will do nothing for you, Evremonde! snapped Defarge. "You are my enemy!"

"Will I Be Left To Rot Unjustly?"

Lucie and Her Father Burst into the Room.

CHAPTER 13

Dr. Manette's New Power

The Tellson's Bank office in Paris was in the wing of a large house. When the Revolution came, the nobleman who owned the house put on his servant's clothes and fled the country.

Mr. Lorry was working late one night when Lucie and her father burst into the room.

"What are you doing in Paris?" he cried. "What is wrong?"

"Charles is here!" gasped Lucie, looking as if she might faint from sheer terror.

"It can't be true!" cried Mr. Lorry.

"Yes, he has been here three — no four — days. He came to help an old servant, but he was stopped at the city gates and sent to the prison of La Force!"

"Then you two will be in danger as well!" cried Mr. Lorry.

"My dear friend," said Dr. Manette calmly, "I do not believe anyone in this city would harm me. In fact, they would welcome me after all of my suffering in the Bastille. That suffering will give me the power to help Charles."

"Then we must speak alone while Lucie goes to my rooms at the back of the bank to rest." And Mr. Lorry ushered Lucie out of the office.

When they were alone Mr. Lorry motioned to Dr. Manette to look out the window. In the courtyard beyond was a huge grindstone being turned by two savage-looking men. Fighting to get close to sharpen their hatchets, knives, and swords were forty or fifty frenzied men, whose blood and sweat mixed with the sparks from the stone.

"What is the meaning of this?" asked the doctor, drawing away from the window.

"What Is the Meaning of This?"

"They are going to murder the prisoners at La Force," said Mr. Lorry. "If you really have the power you think you have, then go out among those savages, tell them who you are, and seek help for Charles! There is no time to spare!"

Hardly were the words out of Mr. Lorry's mouth than the doctor was standing before the grindstone in the courtyard, his white hair streaming in the wind, his eyes gleaming with determination, his arms waving excitedly as he spoke.

Suddenly, a roar went up from the crowd. "Long live the Bastille prisoner! Long live his kin! Save Evremonde from La Force!"

Then the mob surged forward, with Dr. Manette at the front, leading the way to La Force. Mr. Lorry left the window and went to comfort Lucie through the long night ahead.

The next morning, when Dr. Manette had not returned, Mr. Lorry found a small apartment nearby where Lucie, her child, and Miss

Dr. Manette Speaks to the Crowd.

Pross would be more comfortable. Then he hired Jerry Cruncher to guard them.

The day dragged on as Mr. Lorry attended to his duties at the bank, and still there was no word from Dr. Manette. Then, just after closing time, a stranger entered his office.

"Do you know me, Mr. Lorry?" asked the thin, dark-haired man.

"I have seen you somewhere," replied Mr. Lorry, wondering how the man knew his name.

"Perhaps at my wine shop," said Ernest Defarge.

Mr. Lorry's eyes opened wide. "Do you come from Dr. Manette?" he asked eagerly.

Defarge handed him a note from the doctor. It was dated only an hour before and read:

"Charles is safe, but I cannot leave this place yet. The bearer of this message also has a note from Charles to his wife."

"I will take you to his wife," said Mr. Lorry when he had finished reading the note.

As they went out into the courtyard, Mr.

A Note from Dr. Manette

Lorry saw Madame Defarge standing near the grindstone, knitting as she had been when Mr. Lorry had last seen her years before.

"My wife will come with us," said Defarge, "so she can recognize the people we are going to see. It is for their safety."

Mr. Lorry was slightly suspicious of this reasoning, but did not wish to delay.

When Mr. Lorry and the Defarges arrived at the apartment, they found Lucie weeping. She read the brief note from Charles:

"Be brave, darling. I am well, and your father is helping me. Kiss our child for me."

Lucie turned to the Defarges to thank them tearfully, but the cold glare she got in return from Madame Defarge gave her a moment of terror. That terror grew when the glare was turned on her child and Miss Pross as well.

"Come," said Madame Defarge, smiling slyly at her husband. "I have seen them. We can go now."

Dr. Manette did not return from La Force for

A Cold Glare from Madame Defarge!

four days. During that time, eleven hundred prisoners were murdered by the bloodthirsty mobs. During that time also, Dr. Manette had appeared before a self-appointed people's "court," which had been sentencing most prisoners to death, and told of his eighteen years of suffering in the Bastille.

Those members of the court who were not asleep or drunk listened to him, including Ernest Defarge, who backed up his story. The decision was made to spare the prisoner's life, but for his own safety, Charles would have to remain in jail.

Dr. Manette begged for permission to remain too and thus assure himself that Charles would not mistakenly be dragged out and killed by the mob.

On the fourth day, Dr. Manette returned home to bring news to Lucie. And because of his new-found fame, he had been named inspecting doctor of La Force Prison. Thus, in the days, weeks, and months following, he was

Appearing Before a People's "Court"

able to see Charles often and to inform Lucie that he was well. But Dr. Manette could not get Charles freed, or even brought to trial.

The king, however, was tried and found guilty of crimes against the people. His sentence — beheading by the guillotine, that terrible instrument of death created by the Revolution. Its victims were wheeled through the streets in wooden carts amid cheering and jeering mobs and dragged onto the platform. Yes, the guillotine provided great excitement for the bloodthirsty mobs. Would Charles be its next victim?

One evening, upon his return from the prison, Dr. Manette told Lucie that if she stood at a certain place in the road across from La Force at three every afternoon, he could arrange to have Charles at an upper window from which he could see her.

From that time on, Lucie went to the spot every day, in all weather, often with her daughter. She couldn't see Charles, but even if

The Guillotine!

she could, it would have been very dangerous to wave to him. Still, she hoped he saw her.

On that same street where Lucie stood each day was a dark and dirty hut, the home of a woodcutter, who was once a road fixer. After seeing Lucie there day after day, the woodcutter called, "Good afternoon, Citizeness!"

"Good afternoon, Citizen," she replied, using the new words ordered by the Revolution.

"You walk here often, Citizeness!" he said. "But that's none of my business. My business is sawing wood to build guillotines!"

This conversation was repeated every day, with Lucie becoming more and more frightened at the sight of the Revolution's new instrument of death.

One snowy afternoon, Dr. Manette met Lucie on that street and brought her the news: "Charles is being put on trial tomorrow!"

Behind them, rattling through the snow, came the wooden carts, carrying their victims to the guillotine!

"Good Afternoon, Citizeness!"

"We Seek the Citizen Evremonde!"

CHAPTER 14

A Spy Is Unmasked

Dr. Manette and Theophile Gabelle both testified at Charles' trial and managed to convince the bloodthirsty jury of his innocence. By a unanimous vote, Charles was freed.

That evening, Charles was relaxing by the fire with his overjoyed family, when suddenly, a loud knock was heard at the door. Dr. Manette went to answer it.

Four rough men, wearing red caps and carrying pistols and sabers, rushed into the room. "We seek the Citizen Evremonde, called Darnay!" cried one. "He is again a prisoner of the Republic!"

"On what charges?" asked the doctor, frozen in disbelief.

"He has been accused by Saint Antoine!"

"By whom in Saint Antoine?"

"He has been denounced by the Citizen and Citizeness Defarge... and by one other person. I cannot say any more. You will find out the rest tomorrow, when the prisoner is brought to trial. But for now, we must take Citizen Evremonde with us to La Force."

While the arrest was being made, Jerry Cruncher and Miss Pross were out doing the family shopping. On the way home, they turned into a wine shop to make the last of their purchases. No sooner did they cross the doorway than Miss Pross let out a scream that brought all the customers to their feet.

Ignoring them, she ran across the room and embraced a thin, dark-haired man. "Solomon! My brother!" she cried. "It has been years since I heard from you, and now I find you here in Paris!"

"Solomon! My Brother!"

"Don't call me Solomon! Do you want me to be killed?" he said in an urgent whisper. "It is better if we talk outside."

"Aren't you glad to see me?" asked Miss Pross, following the man out the door, with Jerry only a step behind her.

"I knew you were in Paris," said the man, giving her a dutiful kiss on the cheek. "But it is best for you to go your way and I to go mine. I am a respected prison official."

"A prison official? In a foreign country? I'm ashamed of you, Solomon!"

"Enough!" snapped Solomon. "Talk like this can put me under suspicion, even cause my death!"

"Just a minute!" cut in Jerry Cruncher. "You didn't use the name Solomon Pross when you were in England! I recognize you now. You were a witness at Charles Darnay's trial at the Old Bailey! You said your name was John . . . ."

"John Barsad!" interrupted a voice from the

"I'm Ashamed of You!"

darkness. As the owner of the voice drew near he was revealed to be Sidney Carton.

"Do not be alarmed, Miss Pross," said Sidney, "but I have the unpleasant task of telling you that your brother has become a prison spy!"

"What do you know about me?" asked the brother, becoming very pale.

"I was walking outside the prison walls about an hour ago when I saw you coming out," said Sidney. "I have an excellent memory for faces, and I remembered yours, especially since I associate it with the bad luck of one of my close friends. I decided to follow you into this wine shop, where I listened to your conversation with some of your friends. It was then that I realized what your true occupation is... and I suddenly knew that you could serve a purpose for me."

"What purpose?" the spy asked.

"We should not talk about it here," said Sidney. "We will escort your sister to her home

"Your Brother Has Become a Spy!"

and then invite Mr. Cruncher to join us in a little talk in Mr. Lorry's private office."

Realizing that he could not refuse to go without the risk of being exposed, Solomon Pross, alias John Barsad, agreed.

Jarvis Lorry was relaxing by the fire when the three men arrived. His smile of welcome for Sidney and Jerry froze when he recognized John Barsad with them.

Sidney explained, "Mr. Barsad here is the brother that Miss Pross wasted so much love on, who once took her money and left her to fend for herself. But he is not important now. I have other news... bad news. Charles has been arrested again!"

"That's impossible!" cried Mr. Lorry. "I saw him a short while ago with his family."

"Mr. Barsad just told a fellow spy over a bottle of wine that the arrest took place," said Sidney. "But what troubles me, Mr. Lorry, is that Dr. Manette did not have the power to stop this arrest. And he may not be able to do

Mr. Lorry Receives Bad News.

anything tomorrow either, when Charles is put on trial. Therefore, I shall have to depend upon someone else for help, a prison official perhaps? . . . You, Mr. Barsad!"

"And if I refuse to help you? There is no way you can force me!" cried Barsad.

"Force you?" sneered Sidney. "Hardly! You, who are now in the pay of the French Republic, were once in the service of the English Government. Who is to say that you are not, in fact, still spying for England? You, who had one name in England, now go by another in France. What would happen if I denounced you to the revolutionary committee of Saint Antoine? No, Mr. Barsad, I force you to do nothing."

John Barsad fell back into a chair trembling. He had spied in France, first among Englishmen there and later among Frenchmen. Before the Revolution, he had spied in the service of the French king upon the people of Saint Antoine. He had seen Madame Defarge

"I Force You To Do Nothing."

knitting constantly while he was in her husband's wine shop and had since learned that the names of those knitted into her list met death on the guillotine.

"By the way," said Sidney, breaking into the spy's thoughts with the next step in his plan, "who was that fellow spy you were talking to earlier at the wine shop?"

"He's French; you don't know him," Barsad answered quickly.

"He spoke good French, but not like a Frenchman. I know... it was Roger Cly! He was disguised, but I recognized him! He, too, was at the Old Bailey trial!"

"Now you've gone too far!" said Barsad with a sly smile. "Roger Cly, who once *was* a partner of mine, has been dead for several years. In fact, I helped to lay him in his coffin! I just happen to be carrying a copy of his death certificate!" And he pulled out a piece of paper from his pocket.

Suddenly, a remarkable thing happened.

Roger Cly's Death Certificate

Jerry Cruncher rose from his chair. Every hair on his head was standing on end, and a violent expression covered his face. "So you laid Cly in his coffin?" he snarled.

"Yes, I did," insisted Barsad.

"Then who took him out of it? All that was in that coffin was paving stones!"

"How do you know that?" cried Barsad.

"Don't matter how I know, but I'll swear it's true!" growled Jerry.

Sidney Carton now joined in. "So, now you can also be accused in Saint Antoine of having links with another spy working for the English Government. It will look even more suspicious when that spy is seen to have pretended to be dead and then to have come to life again!"

John Barsad saw that he was beaten. "I admit it," he said. "I was hardly able to get out of England without being clubbed to death on the streets, and Roger Cly could only escape by pretending to have died. But I'll never understand how this man here knows about

"So You Laid Cly in His Coffin?"

that coffin and Cly's body!"

"Never mind about that!" snapped Sidney. "Will you go along with what I ask you now?"

"Don't expect too much of me," pleaded Barsad. "I'm not a very important official — only a guard at La Force Prison."

"I only want to know one thing," Sidney persisted. "Do you have keys to the prison cells in your guardhouse?"

"Yes."

"Then I will have to talk to you privately!"

And the two men left the room.

After John Barsad had returned to his jailing and spying duties at La Force, and Sidney Carton had returned to Mr. Lorry's room, the banker asked what arrangements he had made with Barsad.

"Only that if it goes badly with Charles, I will be able to see him one last time."

"Is that all? Seeing him once will not save him from death!" cried Mr. Lorry.

"I know that, but there is nothing more that

"I'm Not a Very Important Official."

you or Dr. Manette can do! Do not ask me what I am planning, sir. Whatever good I am doing will not make up for the worthless life I have led. There is no one to mourn me when I am dead, no one who loved or respected me in my lifetime. I have never done good for anyone in all my years on earth! Maybe now...."

Mr. Lorry looked puzzled at these strange words, but agreed to meet Sidney at the courthouse the following morning.

Once outside the banker's rooms, Sidney walked several blocks to a chemist's shop, where he bought two bottles of liquid.

"Together, they are a very powerful drug," warned the chemist. "Be careful with them!"

Sidney nodded and left. "There is nothing to do now until tomorrow," he said to himself.

After walking the streets all night, Sidney returned to his room at daybreak to wash and dress. He had coffee and bread instead of his usual wine for breakfast, then set out to attend the trial of Charles Darnay.

The Chemist's Warning!

Denounced as an Enemy of the Republic!

CHAPTER 15

Doomed!

"Charles St. Evremonde, known as Darnay," announced the prosecutor. "Freed and retaken. Denounced as an enemy of the Republic, a nobleman, one of a family of tyrants that lived off the blood of the people! "

"Who denounced the prisoner?" the president of the tribunal asked the prosecutor.

"Three people. Ernest Defarge, owner of the wine shop in Saint Antoine."

"Who else?"

"Therese Defarge, his wife."

"Who else?"

"Alexandre Manette, a doctor!"

A great uproar filled the courtroom, and Dr. Manette, pale and trembling, slumped in his seat.

Ernest Defarge was called to the witness box. He told of his youth, serving Dr. Manette, and later of sheltering the doctor after his release from the Bastille.

"What did you do the day that the Bastille fell to the people?" the president asked.

"I ordered a jailer to take me and a fellow citizen, who now sits on the jury, to 105 North Tower, where Dr. Manette had said he lived as a prisoner. In a hole in the chimney of the cell, behind a stone, I found this paper in Dr. Manette's handwriting."

The president read the paper:

"I, Alexandre Manette, write this sad note secretly in my cell in the Bastille, in December, 1767. I will hide it in the chimney, hoping some pitying soul will find it after my death. I write it now, in the tenth year of my imprisonment, for there is no hope of my ever being freed, and

The President Reads Dr. Manette's Letter.

I fear that I will soon lose my mind. But for now, I have all my wits with me, and I swear that my story is the truth.

"On December 22, 1757, I was walking near my house when a carriage drew up behind me and a voice called out my name. Two gentlemen — twin brothers as I later realized — stepped out. They were wrapped in cloaks and carrying weapons. They told me politely but firmly to enter the carriage, and since I was unarmed, I had to obey. I was driven to a house on a lonely country road, where I found a beautiful young woman with brain fever lying on a bed. To keep her from injuring herself in her ravings, her arms were tied to her sides with sashes and handkerchiefs that belonged to a gentleman's wardrobe. They bore the coat of arms of a noble family and the letter 'E'.

"The patient kept shouting, 'My husband, my father, my brother!' and then counting up to twelve and saying, 'Hush!'

Forced To Enter a Carriage

"Since I had left my medicine bag at home when I went for my walk that night, the brothers gave me some drugs with which to quiet the patient.

" 'Does she have a husband, a father, and a brother?" I asked one of the twins.

" 'A brother,' he answered, 'who is also a patient here for you to see.' And he led me to a loft by the stable, where I found a handsome peasant boy, about seventeen years old, lying in some hay.

"The boy was dying of a stab wound, and although he gritted his teeth in pain, he wouldn't let me examine the wound. But it was too late to save his life anyhow.

" 'How did this happen?' I asked one of the twins, whom I shall call the younger.

" 'A crazy young common dog,' he spat. 'A slave! He forced my brother to stab him.'

" 'These noblemen rob us, beat us, and kill us!' gasped the boy, gathering his strength so he could tell his story before he died. 'But

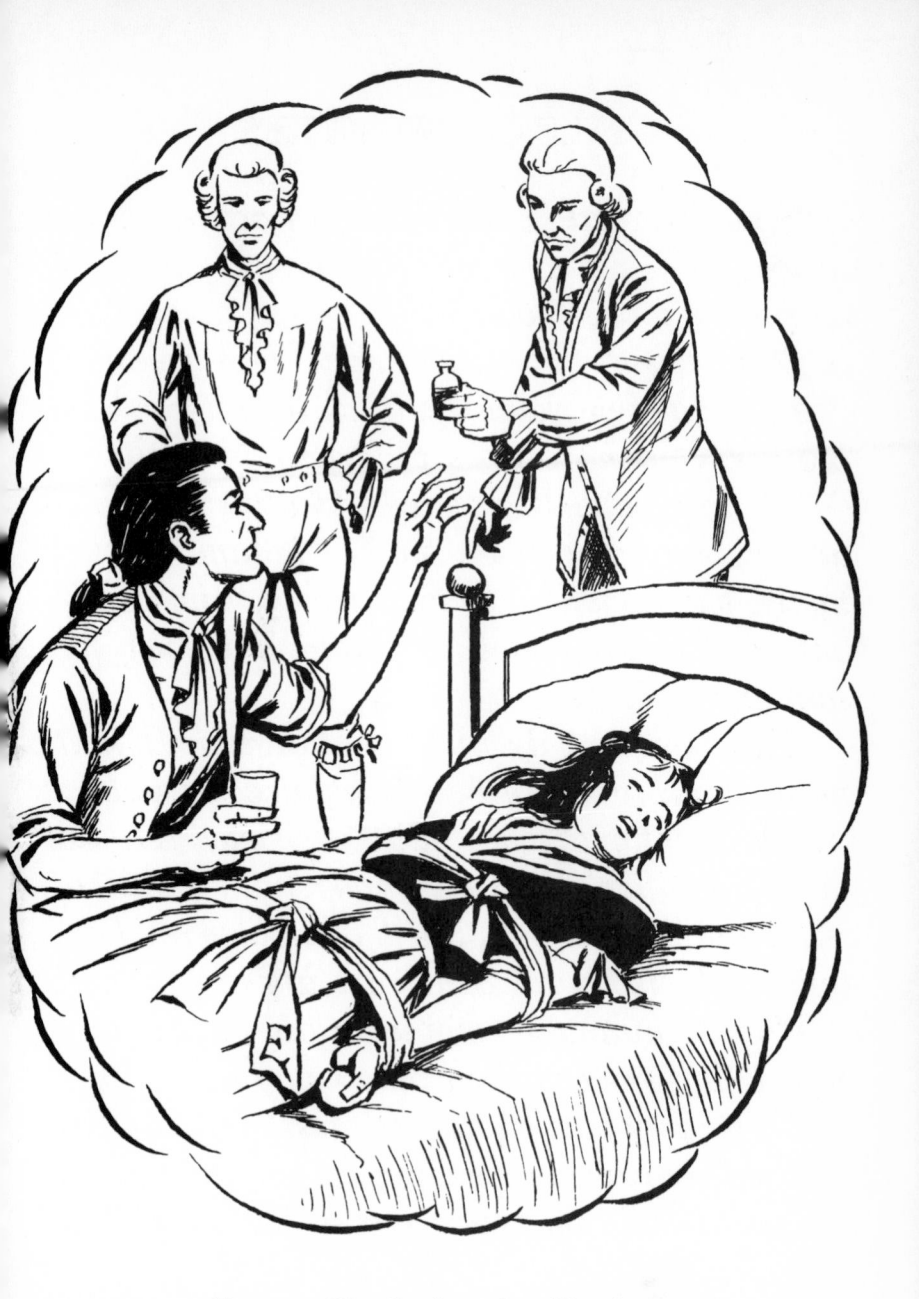

Drugs To Quiet the Patient

we have our pride. Have you seen my sister, doctor?'

" '*Yes,' I answered.*

" '*She was a good girl. She was engaged to marry a nice young man, a tenant of these two noblemen. We were all tenants — almost slaves. They taxed us, forced us to work without pay, took our crops for their animals, and barely fed us enough to keep us alive! But even worse, they took our young women for their own pleasure.*

" '*Right after my sister got married, that man's twin brother ordered her husband to give her to him for a while. But my sister refused to go with him. And her husband refused to persuade her to do so. So that nobleman harnessed her husband to a cart like an animal and drove him over the estate day after day, beating him to keep him moving. When he was finally taken out of the harness one day at noon to look for something to eat he sobbed twelve times — one for every stroke of the bell*

Listening to the Dying Boy's Story

— then collapsed and died in my sister's arms.

" 'Then that man's brother took my sister away for his pleasure. When I told my father it broke his heart. I immediately took my younger sister—for I have another—to a place beyond the reach of this man. Last night I tracked the older brother here and climbed in the window, sword in hand. He came at me with his whip, and my sister ran to us. I told her not to come near us until he was dead.*

" 'I struck at him to make him draw his sword. Lift me up now, doctor, so that I can see this evil man.'

"I raised him in my arms. He turned to the younger twin and said, 'Marquis, when the time comes that your crimes will be answered for, I call upon you and your brother, the last of your evil race, to answer for them. I mark this cross of blood upon both of you as a sign.'

"The dying boy put his hand to his wound and with his bloody forefinger drew a cross in the air. Then his finger dropped, his body went

"I Climbed in the Window, Sword in Hand."

limp, and I laid him down dead. . . .

"When I returned home, I had to unburden myself of the terrible secret and I decided to write to the minister at the king's court, explaining what had happened.

"I had just finished the letter when a beautiful young lady, looking ill and very upset, came to my door. She said she was the wife of the Marquis St. Evremonde. I connected that name with the name by which the dying boy addressed one of the twin brothers and with the initial 'E' on the handkerchief.

"The lady had discovered her husband's part in the story I have just written down. She felt pity for the dead girl and not only wanted to help her family, but also turn the anger of Heaven away from the Evremonde family, which was so hated by the people of France.

"She also wanted to reach the younger sister, but I could not tell her the girl's name or address, for the wounded boy never revealed it before he died.

A Visit from the Wife of the Marquis

"The lady had a pretty child with her — a boy about two or three years old.

" 'For his sake, doctor,' she begged, 'for the sake of little Charles, I want to do anything I can to make up for my husband's evil deeds. For I fear if I do not, one day Charles may have to pay for his father's crimes. What I have left in this world to call my own — only a few jewels — I would like to give the injured family, if the sister can be found.'

"After she left I delivered my letter to the king's court. That very night December 31, a man in black rang my doorbell and told my young servant, Ernest Defarge, that there was a medical emergency and that he had brought a coach to take me to the patient. Ernest summoned me, and I agreed to go.

"As soon as I was out of the house, the man in black tied a black muffler over my mouth and pinned my arms to my sides. The brothers Evremonde ran out from a dark corner and with a nod, identified me. One of them was

Pleading for Help, for Her Child's Sake!

holding the letter I had written to the king's court.

"The coach brought me here to the Bastille — to my living grave. And in all these years, the brothers never found it in their hearts even to bring me news whether my dear wife was alive or dead. For this I denounce them and their heirs, to the last of their race. I, Alexandre Manette, unhappy prisoner, on this last night of the year 1767, do denounce them until the time when all these crimes shall be answered for."

A dreadful roar arose in the courtroom when the president of the tribunal finished reading. The vote of the jury was as solidly against Charles Darnay as it had been in his favor the last time. Death by the guillotine in twenty-four hours!

Forced into a Coach!

Noticing a Strong Resemblance

CHAPTER 16

A Fateful Meeting

After Sidney Carton took Lucie and Dr. Manette home from the courthouse, he left them in the care of Mr. Lorry and Miss Pross, and turned his steps toward Saint Antoine and to Ernest Defarge's wine shop.

Madame Defarge served the Englishman his wine and listened to him struggling to make himself understood in French (a tongue which Sidney spoke well). Returning to the counter, she remarked to her husband how much Sidney looked like Charles St. Evremonde.

Defarge looked at Sidney, nodded to his wife, then returned to his conversation with the only other customer in the shop — Jacques Three. "We must stop somewhere," Defarge said loudly, confident that his French was not understood by the Englishman at the table.

"We can't stop short of execution!" cried his wife.

"Execution is a good thing," added Jacques. "Our enemies should be put to death!"

"But Dr. Manette has suffered so much already," said Defarge, "and so has his daughter."

"If I left it up to you, you would try to save the prisoner even now," complained Madame Defarge. "But I knitted the Evremonde family into my list a long time ago. They must all be destroyed — Lucie and the child as well!"

"Why are you so bitter against the wife and child, Madame?" asked Jacques Three.

"When the Bastille fell, Jacques, my husband found that paper in the North Tower, and we read Dr. Manette's story together. My reaction was one of horror for, you see, that

"I Knitted the Family into My List."

peasant family described in it was *my* family. That slain boy was *my* brother, that kidnapped girl dying of brain fever was *my* sister, their heartbroken father was *my* father! I am the only surviving member of that family, and the duty to avenge the crimes of the Evremondes — every last one — falls upon me."

Other customers entered the wine shop, and the conversation stopped.

Sidney had overheard enough. Now Lucie and the child were in danger as well. He had to act quickly.

Leaving the shop, he headed for Mr. Lorry's room for a planned meeting at nine o'clock with the banker and Dr. Manette. But it wasn't until the clock was striking midnight that the old doctor appeared at the door. The look on his face made it clear to Sidney and Mr. Lorry that all was lost!

"I can't find it! Where is it?" cried the doctor, tearing wildly at his hair. "I must have my

"That Peasant Family Was *My* Family."

shoemaker's bench and tools!"

All was lost, utterly lost!

The two men soothed the weeping doctor and assured him that he would have his tools shortly. Sidney then pulled a piece of paper from his pocket and searched through the doctor's pockets until he found a similar one. Handing them both to Mr. Lorry, he explained, "These travel papers will allow Lucie, Dr. Manette, the child, and me to leave Paris. Hold them for me until tomorrow, for I do not wish to carry them with me when I go into the prison. You and I are Englishmen and will be able to leave Paris safely, but I have reason to believe that the travel papers for the doctor and Lucie and the child may be canceled if we do not hurry!"

"Are they in danger?" asked Mr. Lorry.

"In great danger, sir. Just tonight, I heard Madame Defarge make plans to denounce them. But you, Mr. Lorry, can save them all!"

"I would do anything for them!"

Sidney Gives Mr. Lorry Travel Papers.

"Have a coach ready to leave Paris at two o'clock tomorrow afternoon. Tell Lucie of the danger they are in and that for the sake of her child and her father, she must go with you. Tell her this was her husband's final wish. Be in the coach with them all and keep a place for me. As soon as I arrive, pull me inside and drive away. Just be sure you have all the papers with you so we can all leave for England. And no matter what happens, you must not change your plans!"

"You are a fine man to help them this way," said Jarvis Lorry, taking Sidney's hand eagerly. "I will do as you ask."

The two men then escorted the old doctor home, and afterwards, Sidney stood in the darkened street looking up at Lucie's lighted window. "May Heaven bless you," he whispered. "Farewell, my love. . . ."

While Sidney was making his plans, Charles was alone in his prison cell, writing his final letters. He reassured Lucie of his love for her

"Farewell, My Love. . . ."

and begged her to be strong for her father's sake; he asked Dr. Manette to take care of his wife and child; and he thanked Mr. Lorry for his friendship and entrusted him with his business affairs. He never thought of Sidney Carton in his final hours.

The clock struck two. In another hour, the prisoner would be dragged to a wooden cart for the ride to the guillotine.

Suddenly the key turned in the lock, and a jailer opened the door. Sidney Carton entered the cell, and Charles jumped to his feet.

"I come with a request from Lucie," said Sidney. "There is no time to explain. Just take off your jacket and tie and boots, and put on mine. And give me the ribbon from your hair and shake it out loose like mine."

When Charles did not move to obey, Carton began forcing the changes on him.

"Carton, this is madness!" cried Charles. "Nobody can escape from here! You will only die with me!"

"Nobody Can Escape from Here!"

"I didn't ask you to try to escape. Just sit here and write what I tell you to," ordered Carton, as he forced Charles into a chair and pushed a pen into his hands.

"To whom do I address it?" asked Charles, pressing his hand to his bewildered head.

"To no one," replied Sidney. And he stood behind Charles, his hand slowly creeping inside his shirt. "Now write this: 'If you remember the words that passed between us long ago, you will understand what I am doing. . . .' "

"I smell something strange in the room," said Charles, unable to see Sidney's hand slowly coming out of his shirt.

"I do not smell anything," said Sidney calmly. "Keep on writing: 'I am thankful to get the chance to prove those words I said to you so long ago—that I would lay down my life for you. I do it now eagerly, and you are to have no grief, no regret. . . .' "

Charles' eyes became clouded, and his

"Keep On Writing."

fingers dropped the pen. At that moment, Sidney's hand, wrapped around the cloth soaked with the chemist's liquid, pressed hard against Charles' nose, while his other hand grabbed him around the chest. For a few seconds, Charles struggled, then he lay unconscious on the ground, at the feet of the man who had come to lay down his life for him.

Sidney quickly put on Charles' clothes and tied his hair back with the ribbon.

"Guard!" called Sidney, and John Barsad entered the cell. "Take my visitor out; he has become ill." Then in a whisper, he added, "Carry him to his coach and take him immediately to Mr. Lorry at the place of our plans. Keep your end of the deal, Barsad, and my lips will be sealed forever."

Barsad carried Charles out, and Sidney was alone.

The clock struck three, and a guard entered. "Follow me, Evremonde!" he ordered. "The guillotine awaits!"

"Take My Visitor Out."

Passing Travel Papers to a Guard

CHAPTER 17

Fleeing the Revolution

Just before three that afternoon, a carriage going out of Paris stopped at the city gates.

"Your travel papers," demanded a guard.

The papers were passed out of the carriage, and the guard read: "Alexandre Manette. Doctor. French. Which passenger is he?"

Jarvis Lorry pointed to a helpless, murmuring old man. "This is he."

"The Citizen Doctor doesn't seem to be in his right mind," said the guard. "The fever of the Revolution must be too much for him. . . . Lucie. His daughter. French. The wife of Evremonde, I believe?"

"She is," replied Mr. Lorry.

"The same Evremonde who has a date with the guillotine," sneered the guard. "Then there is Lucie. Her child. English. . . . And Sidney Carton. Lawyer. English. Which is he?"

"Here," said Mr. Lorry, pointing to an unconscious figure slumped in the corner of the carriage. "He has been in poor health and has just come from a sad parting from a friend who is in trouble with the Republic. "

"And last, Jarvis Lorry. Banker. English."

"I am Jarvis Lorry. . . . May we leave Paris now, Citizen?"

"Yes, here are your papers, signed and ready," said the guard. "Have a good journey!

"He Has Been in Poor Health."

Madame Defarge's Secret Plotting

CHAPTER 18

Outwitting the Guillotine

As the guillotine awaited its victims that day, Madame Defarge met with Jacques Two and Jacques Three. She had chosen Jacques Two's woodcutter's hut near the prison for the meeting, rather than the wine shop.

"I am here alone," she explained to them, "because while my husband is a good Republican and a brave man, he feels sorry for the doctor. I myself care nothing for Dr. Manette, alive or dead! But the Evremonde family must be destroyed; the wife and child must follow the husband and father to the guillotine!"

"What a pretty sight that would be!" croaked the men, rubbing their hands in glee.

"But I cannot trust my husband in this matter. If he knew of my plans, he might even warn them so they could escape. I need your help, Citizen woodcutter. Will you testify in court that you saw Evremonde's wife making signs to the prisoners from the road?"

"Certainly! I saw her standing there every afternoon for months, sometimes with the child, and once, even with her father. Clearly she was plotting with the prisoners against the Republic!"

"Will the jury go along?" she asked Jacques Three, who was a member of the Tribunal's jury.

"You can count on the jury!" he assured her.

"I really cannot let the doctor go free, even for my husband's sake," added Madame Defarge. "The guillotine needs more heads! Meet me in Saint Antoine tonight, and we will denounce them all. In the meanwhile, I want

"I Saw Her Standing There. . . ."

to see Evremonde's wife while she is mourning his death sentence and is full of anger against the Republic. She will surely speak of her hatred for the Revolution, and that will serve as more evidence against her at her trial. I will meet you at my usual chair at the guillotine."

And with a pistol hidden in her dress and a dagger in her belt, Madame Defarge left the hut and made her way to the Manette house.

Mr. Lorry had arranged for Miss Pross and Jerry Cruncher to follow them minutes later in another, smaller carriage, since the first one could only hold the five travelers whose escape was more urgent.

Jerry had gone out to bring round the carriage, and as Miss Pross was about to leave, the door burst open and Madame Defarge stormed in.

"Where is the wife of Evremonde?" she demanded.

Miss Pross moved to block the doorway to Lucie's room, knowing that the longer she kept

"Where Is the Wife of Evremonde?"

the French woman here, the more time her dear Lucie would have to escape. "You are a hard woman," said Miss Pross, "but I am harder. I know of your evil plans, but you won't succeed."

Madame peered into the three rooms whose doors stood open. All were empty. Then she lunged at the door Miss Pross was blocking, but the English woman grabbed her around the waist, locking in the dagger hidden in her belt.

Unable to struggle out of the strangling hold of the powerful woman, Madame Defarge reached into her blouse and seized the pistol. But she was not quick enough, for Miss Pross struck at it. There was a flash, then a shot, and through the smoke Miss Pross saw the body of Madame Defarge lying dead at her feet!

As the coach carrying Miss Pross and Jerry left Paris the wooden carts bringing the day's fifty-two prisoners arrived at the guillotine.

Miss Pross Strikes First!

"There is Evremonde!" shouted someone in the crowd.

"Down with all aristocrats! " shouted others.

Many women sat knitting as they watched and counted the heads drop from the guillotine. One of these women looked around at the empty chair near her. "Where is Therese Defarge?" she cried. "She never misses executions! And surely not this one!"

Sidney Carton was number twenty-three. As his cart rumbled toward the platform, he turned his eyes toward Heaven and whispered, "I see my dear friends for whom I am giving my life living peaceful, useful, happy lives. I see them holding a special place for me in their hearts, remembering me with love, as no one ever did before. Yes, this is a far, far better thing that I am doing than anything I have ever done in my life. The eternal rest that I am going to will be a far, far better rest than any I have ever known. . . ."

"This is a Far, Far Better Thing . . . ."